The Goodnight Train

JuNe SoBeL

Illustrated by LauRa HuliskA-BeitH

Harcourt, Inc.

Orlando   Austin   New York   San Diego   Toronto   London

For information about permission to reproduce selections from this
book, please write Permissions, Houghton Mifflin Harcourt Publishing
Company 215 Park Avenue South NY NY 10003.

www.hmhbooks.com

Library of Congress Cataloging-in-Publication Data
Sobel, June.
The Goodnight Train/by June Sobel:
illustrated by Laura Huliska-Beith.
p. cm.
Summary: A child's bedtime ritual follows the imaginary
journey of a goodnight train's trip to the Dreamland station.
[1. Bedtime—Fiction. 2. Railroads—Trains—Fiction.
3. Stories in rhyme.] I. Title: Goodnight Train.
II. Huliska-Beith, Laura, ill. III. Title.
PZ8.3.S692Go 2006
[E]—dc22   2004025169
ISBN-13: 978-0-15-205436-6 ISBN-10: 0-15-205436-7

SCP 13 12
4500399022

Printed in China

The illustrations in this book were done in
acrylic paints with fabric and paper collage.
The display lettering was created by Laura Huliska-Beith.
The text type was set in Pink Martini.
Color separations by Colourscan Co., Pte., Ltd., Singapore
Printed and bound by South China Printing
Production supervision by Pascha Gerlinger
Designed by April Ward

To the memory of Clara Sobel,
who loved the world of books.
—J. S.

For Amelie, the newlywed, and Betty,
the newly graduated. Here's to new love,
new adventures, and more naps.
—L. H. B.

The Goodnight Train gets set to roll.
It's being shined and filled with coal.

Wash the cars off with a hose.
Scrub the engine's dirty nose.

Scrub-a-dub! Scrub-a-dub! Toot! Toot!

All aboard! The sun is down.
The Goodnight Train is leaving town.

Find your sleepers! Grab your teddy.
Climb right up! Your bed is ready!

"All tucked in," the porter cries.
"Pillows fluffed. Now close your eyes."

WHOO

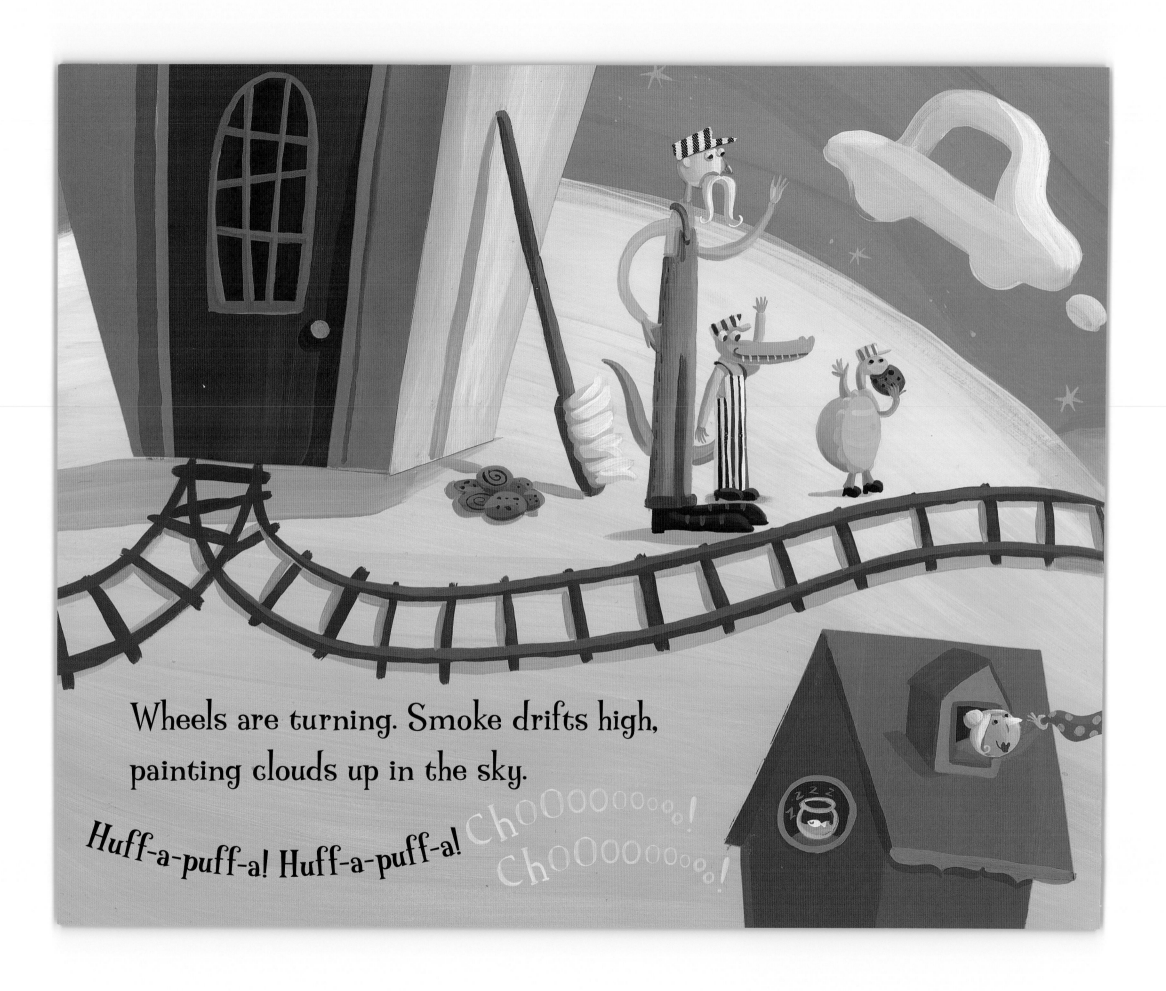

Wheels are turning. Smoke drifts high,
painting clouds up in the sky.

Huff-a-puff-a! Huff-a-puff-a! ChOOOOooooo!
ChOOOOOooooo!

Slumber, lumber up the hill.
Cars climb slowly up until…

Roll the corner, rock the curve.
Blankets bounce with every swerve.

Rock-a, rock-a, rock-a, rock-a—

Shhhhhhhhhh!
Shhhhhhhhhh!

Fly through a tunnel black as ink—
in and out before you blink.

Snnnoorrre
Diner
PROFESSIONAL
BEDBUG
REMOVAL!
CALL FOR
FREE ESTIMATE

Catch that freight train whizzing past!
The Goodnight Train is moving fast!

Cars sway on the wooden track.
Wheels go click. Wheels go clack.

Glide across a plain so flat.
Gently toss this way and that.

CLICKETY-CLACK!

CLICKETY-CLACK!

CLICKETY-CLACK!

Curl through farms of fuzzy sheep.
The sleepy train slows to a creep.

Pushing toward the station's light,
cars crawl on with all their might.

Chug...chug...Chug!

"Sweet dreams ahead," the porter sighs.
The tired train can close its eyes.

Home at last, tucked in and snug,
the engine snores a final "Chug!"

Hush-a, hush-a, hush-a, hush-a— *Sleeeeeeeeeep!*

Good night, train.
Good night.